The Monkey and
the Mango

STORIES OF MY GRANNY

by Eknath Easwaran

NILGIRI PRESS

©1996 by the Blue Mountain Center of Meditation

Second printing July 1997

The Blue Mountain Center of Meditation,
founded in Berkeley, California, in 1961
by Eknath Easwaran, publishes books on how to lead
the spiritual life in the home and the community.
For more information please write to
Nilgiri Press, Box 256, Tomales, California 94971

I S B N *0–915132–82–6 : $14.95*
Printed in Hong Kong by
South China Printing Co. (1998) Ltd.

Table of Contents

My Granny

My grandmother was the wisest person I have ever known. She was always aware of the Lord of Love within her, and within every other person and creature around us in the beautiful village in Kerala, South India, where I grew up.

Granny was teaching me at all times. Every evening we used to sit together on the wide veranda of our ancestral home and she would tell me stories from our scriptures – stories that have been told for thousands of years, which teach us that the Lord is one, though we worship him by many names – Krishna, Shiva, Devi, Ganesha – and dwells in every heart.

But Granny taught me at other times as well. Often she would use something from our everyday life to show me the world through her eyes. She revered the elephant because the Lord lives in him as Ganesha, who removes all obstacles. She revered the eagle because in our scriptures it is he who carries the Lord as Krishna on his back. Her whole world was full of God.

In this book, I have written down some of these stories as I remember them from long ago. I hope they will help you, too, to enter my Granny's world, the most wonderful I have known.

Saved at Dawn

There is a pretty pond in front of our family temple where Granny and Mother used to have their bath when dawn was breaking.

Granny was a fine swimmer, but Mother did not swim at all. One morning, as Granny turned her back to go up the steps to get the sandalwood soap, Mother slipped into deep water. "Help! Help!" she cried.

Before Granny could reach her, a strong black arm pulled Mother out of danger. Granny shed tears of devotion because it was a baby elephant that had come to the rescue – a baby elephant that was having his bath at the same time.

"Ganesha be praised! The Lord has saved my daughter," said Granny.

Fireflies

One night I went with Granny and Mother to the temple for a special service in honor of my aunt, who was expecting her first baby. The night was very dark on our return, and I was afraid of stepping on snakes.

Granny understood my fear and sang a nursery rhyme:

> *"Firefly, firefly,*
> *Come with your friends,*
> *And bring a hundred little lights*
> *To show my boy the path."*

As Granny was singing, a swarm of fireflies came toward us and settled on our heads and shoulders.

I was so thrilled by this that I exclaimed, "Granny, you can work miracles!"

She laughed and whispered, "I saw them coming and told them to take away your fears."

The Squirrel Shows His Teeth

Whenever I had to lose one of my baby teeth during childhood, Granny would ask me to sit on our veranda in the early morning, when the birds were singing in the mango trees. Then she would make the chattering sound of a squirrel, and soon one or two would appear on the wall around the nearby shrine.

"Now smile," Granny would tell them, and they would show their pearly teeth.

"Look at that," she would say to me. "May you have teeth like those!"

And while I silently repeated the name of the Lord and watched the squirrels, Granny would gently pull out the loose tooth.

Then she would treat the squirrels to a bowl of puffed rice in return for their dental assistance.

The Mongoose

One day I followed my grandmother along the little paths through our rice fields to the farmhouse. There we found a lot of snakes.

"Can't we get rid of these, Granny? I am afraid of them!"

She did not say anything in reply, which meant she was going to act.

The farm worker was her friend. She asked him to show me his pet mongoose. When he put it down, we watched it run round and round the farmhouse. It chased all the snakes away.

"That is how the name of the Lord chases fear from your mind," Granny said.

The Red Ants

We had a lot of red ants one summer. They bit babies, they bit grown-ups, they even bit dogs and cats. They spared no one.

"I wish, Granny, that God had never created red ants."

She did not say anything, but bided her time.

The summer gave way to the monsoon, and the rains broke down the raised mud paths that ran through the rice fields. The streams of flowing water looked to me like little canals, but to an ant they must have looked like raging rivers.

"What are the ants going to do, Granny?"

"Just watch," she said.

The red ants made themselves into a ball. The ball grew bigger and bigger and bigger. When all the ants were in the ball, it jumped into the water and floated to the other side. There it unrolled and became many, many ants again.

"God loves all his creatures," Granny said.

The Scorpion's Friend

I had a boyhood friend who wasn't good at school but was very good with scorpions.

"How did you make friends with scorpions, Perumal?" I asked. "The rest of us are afraid of them."

"When I was little," he said, "I rescued a baby scorpion that was drowning. After that, whenever a scorpion fell from the mango tree, I would rescue it. They never stung me at all. Now I can put them in my palm and watch them go to sleep there."

When I told this to Granny, she smiled and said, "When we trust, we get trust in return."

The Golden Eagle and the Silver Snake

Every evening Granny used to stand near the lotus pond looking out over the green rice fields. She was waiting for the golden eagle that carries the Lord on his back. If Granny could not see this sacred eagle, she would go without her dinner.

While the light was fading one evening, Granny was about to return home when the golden eagle swooped by in a hurry. Granny greeted him with devotion because he is the carrier of Lord Krishna. As she did so, a young cobra, pale like silver, wrapped round her ankle for protection from the eagle's sharp claws.

"Oh, Krishna," Granny prayed, "don't let your golden eagle hurt this silver snake."

After the eagle flew away, she said to the young cobra, "You are safe now. But promise to tell all the snakes not to harm my boy when he comes home after dark."

The Secret Cranny

In the room where I was born, there was a secret cranny near the ceiling in which Mother kept her jewelry. "When I grow tall," I would tell her, "I am going to see what treasures are hidden there."

I had to wait a few years before I grew tall enough to put my fingers into the secret hiding place. Imagine my joy when her big gold Kerala earrings came into my hand . . . followed by a pair of bicycle clips.

"Why would Mother want to keep a pair of old bicycle clips along with her costly earrings?" I asked Granny.

"Your father used to wear them when he rode his bicycle," Granny replied. "They are as precious to your mother as all her fine jewelry."

The Tumbler Pigeon

One day the biggest pigeon I had ever seen landed on our roof. My cousin and I crept up onto the rafters and caught him. We tied his wings with a thread while we made friends with him, and after a few days, let him go. He rose straight up – high, high above the coconut palms – and turned one, two, three somersaults before flying back to us.

The pigeon and I became the best of friends. Every day, when I ran home from school for lunch, he would swoop down and ride on my shoulder into the kitchen, and Granny would feed us both.

Then one morning my pigeon flew away. He flew higher and higher and disappeared into a deep blue monsoon cloud. He did not return.

That night I did not feel like eating my dinner and could not go to sleep. Granny told me, "Everything flies away someday, son. Don't try to hold on, for it leads to sorrow. Some other boy is playing with him now."

The Monkey and the Mango

We had a tall mango tree in our backyard. It gave us only a few fruits, but they were delicious.

One afternoon when I came home from school, I told Granny I was hungry. She pointed out a big mango, red and yellow, on the topmost branch of the mango tree. But there was no way I could climb to such a height.

"Look up!" Granny said.

Right above the mango I saw a monkey.

"Pick up a pebble and throw it at him," she said. I did, and missed him with a yard to spare. But the monkey pulled off the mango and threw it back at me. I caught it.

Granny left a bowl of peanuts for the monkey, and we went in to enjoy the mango.